LONDON INDEPENDENT
WINNERS & FINALISTS
5TH ANNIVERSARY
ANTHOLOGY
SHORT STORY – FLASH FICTION - POETRY

LISP
LONDON
INDEPENDENT
STORY PRIZE

2023

First published in Great Britain
by the London Independent Story Prize, 2023
e.info: entry@londonindependentstoryprize.co.uk
www.londonindependentstoryprize.co.uk
Follow us on Twitter and Instagram @Londonisp
www.facebook.com/LIStoryPrize

ISBN 978-1-7384671-0-5
British Library Cataloguing-in-Publication Data
A catalogue record of this book is available from
the British Library.

Edited by Ozge Gozturk
Cover art by Samantha Sanderson-Marshall,
Smash Design and Illustrations

LISP
LONDON
INDEPENDENT
STORY PRIZE

Table of Contents

Introduction

London Independent Story Prize (LISP) is a not-for-profit organisation founded by storytellers for storytellers. LISP aims to nurture brave voices and create sustainable networking opportunities for writers and filmmakers. Our purpose is to build a community that embraces multicultural differences, bold voices, unique writers, and extraordinary artistic approaches to storytelling.

The stories compiled in this anthology were selected from the LISP 2023 competition. Aligning with LISP's core strategies, these stories are not proofread, edited or polished by professional editors and proofreaders. We acknowledge that language skills, such as grammar and spelling, are linked to access to education. Therefore, LISP does not seek excellence in those elements but values the distinct voice of the writer, the originality of the stories and braveness in the storytelling techniques the most.

Enjoy reading these fantastic stories and poems.

Foreword, Amal Chatterjee

Short stories, poems, flash fiction are intense bursts of light, illuminating places, people, ideas. It's a privilege to read these, the aching pain of "Let Him Bury His Face in The Dust", its telling of drought and loss, "Now as she's leaving, she's as distant as the promise of rain."; the shock of assault, the poignancy of memory, imagination and loss again in "Before the Gale" as "She remembers how as a child she'd talk to daisies and the daisies would talk back in high-pitched voices which sounded like singing"; and the beauty of"my Mare Nostrum/quavers of algae/frond my skin, dissolve the signature of time" in "Sea major". Each of these resonates, they reach into the reader, tap into who we are, what we feel, draw us into worlds and spaces that are at once familiar and new. That's what writing does, it transports us, back to the familiar and out to the new, makes them tangible, alive again. These three writers do just that, they take us on journeys, each in their own way, from the arid wasting in "Let Him Bury His Face in The Dust", to the loss of people, places, letters, the sharpness of remembrance in "Before the Gale", and memory again, the engaging of all the senses in "Sea major".

Reading these reminds me of what writing can do for us as writers - and does. It allows us to spread out beyond where we are, to do things, to delve deep and wide. For ourselves, first, because writing is something one does on one's own, for oneself first. The act of writing, of creating, re-creating, revising, polishing, makes us makers of worlds, great and small. Because whether we invent new or render the known, what appears on the page is what we see, a reality composed of those words. Yes, related to the world around us but that came from within us. That's its first place, writing has that power, the power to make us creators. That's why we write, not (just) for rewards, be they prizes, publication or awards, yes, they have their place as recognition but the fundamental vitality of the written word is its ability to evoke, in the writer as much as the reader. When we write, we create, when we read, we create again. And as we write and re-write, read our work back, what we create becomes as real to us. Writing makes us whole. Congratulations to all these writers, and many thanks to them too.

LISP 2023 Poetry Winner
Karina Fiorini

Sea major

I leave the shoreline
and dive the waters of
Comino, karst murmurs
                    meet the blue saddled
                    bream, it frisks me
          into aromas of sand ripples
          into foraminifera memories,
                    marine cumin perfumes
                    my Mare Nostrum,
                              quavers of algae
                              frond my skin, dissolve
                              the signature of time

LISP 2023 Flash Fiction Winner

Gillian O'Shaughnessy

Let Him Bury His Face in the Dust

He'll help her stack her suitcases in the car. Soon, she'll disappear down the endless gravel driveway, miles of it, lined with ash trees that cling to their patch of red earth like spindle-legged spiders, gasping their thirst. He'll stare at them over his wife's head, and he'll think, not for the first time, they should've planted ghost gum or eucalyptus. Trees that sink in their roots and stay while others wither like ill-bred sheep, crusted and fly-blown, left in the dirt while the strong move on.

He saw this coming when they lost their baby girl during the last drought. Slight little thing, she slid from her mother's womb, lay in her arms, still and cold and pale as a moonflower. He watched without words as his wife cried and kissed her sweet face, her paper eyelids, each tiny milk-blue fingernail. Maybe for the best, he'd thought. This salted air, it cuts tender lungs and sears soft skin. He knows better than anyone. He didn't say it hurt him too and soon his wife stopped asking.

Now as she's leaving, she's as distant as the promise of rain. And he drops his eyes before her and stares down at his hands. They're a man's hands, capable in the paddocks, gentle with the ewes when they're lambing, sure as steel when he's shearing or guiding the sheep through the drench, strong when he's pinning a ram between his knees for a swift clean cut to the throat. Or steady on the trigger of his rifle, on relentless marches through the paddocks because there's no water and there won't be tomorrow and even the strongest might stagger and lie in the dust with dull eyes begging for a merciful end. They never see it coming. They don't feel anything at all.

LISP 2023 Short Story Winner
Jess Richards

Before the Gale

Melanie sits on a bench at the waterfront, looking out to sea. The cargo boats are carrying away metal containers. It's dawn, and her eyes run from the effort of staring for so long, looking for something light, something possible, something which might change. It's only the dawn which conjures this kind of melancholy. What an unreal word, Melancholy. A good name for a sadness-relieving pet. She often seeks out this particular shade of melancholy—if it were a colour, it would be pale lilac. But to deliberately seek it, it has to be there inside her already, doesn't it? Melanie-melancholy. She has pale lilac thoughts.

Rummaging in her handbag, she pulls out a handkerchief. A white square, the corners embroidered with autumn leaves. She wipes tears from the creases beneath her eyes and looks closely at the fabric. The warp and the weft of the linen. What would any one set of lines be, without the other?

A blonde man runs along the waterfront, and there's the sound of a dog panting to keep up with him. As he's about to pass her, she catches his eye and he slows down. She waits for him to tell her to cheer up, the way strangers often do when she's near the ocean and not smiling.

But instead, he jogs on the spot, smiling like some high-rising sun, considering her for a while.

He says, "The stars still shine, whether you them or not." He runs onwards, away.

Melanie murmurs, "Jog on then, wise sodding sage." She listens for the dog but it's gone.

Strangers are odd like that, when she's alone, and they're alone. They say a one-liner, and go away quick. She's left wondering what they meant. It's rude. Speaking with such apparent significance, and leaving.

The cargo boats glide away, no rush, as if they're travelling all the way to the moon. What are in those metal containers? Household possessions, boxes of recycled clothing, guns and bullets? What might the moon have ordered online, from the earth? Bottles of sparkling water? Rose shrubs? Sunflower seeds?

So many things are impossible to know. She puts the handkerchief away in her handbag, and clips it shut. Her grandmother gave her the handkerchief when she was a child. She'd embroidered it herself, and was displeased whenever she saw the linen dirtied.

The last star which lingers above the horizon line is beautiful and strange. She whispers to it, "I wish I didn't remember so much. There are only so many things a mind can contain. I wish I'd spent far more time with pale-lilac thoughts, simply imagining."

Melanie remembers visiting her grandmother in her country cottage the year her grandmother was dying, and she remembers the desperate look in her eyes. She remembers her grandmother's fears: of foreigners, of war, of stains. She remembers her grandmother's apron, and a smear of blood from a butchered lamb. She remembers that lamb alive, and its name was Milly. Milly trembled when she was cold. She remembers announcements on old radios in accents which sounded like posh dolls talking about mass graves and child murders and explosions and fault and blame, and so many reports were about people who'd died or as good as. There was never any good news on the radio, or if there was, it's fallen through some memory-hole.

M-e-m- -r-y-h- -l-e.

Where've they gone?

o o

That's better.

The last star glows brighter.

Surely at dawn it should dim, or blink and go out?

Melanie remembers the time her mum told her she was bad for lying, and about black spots on the soul. She remembers examining the grubby undersides of her small feet, one at a time. She remembers the first time she got her heart broken, and the sweet lips of the girl who broke it. She remembers the violent man she met one night who shoved her up against a wall and hurt her between the legs. She remembers her first girlfriend crying about being abused as a child, saying 'I'll never get over it.' She remembers three friends she'd had as a teenager who died, Tracy from leukaemia, Alex from an overdose and Didd for the maker, from glue-sniffing.

The sky is so much lighter, surely the unblinking star can't last much longer.

Her wife Ada will be at home asleep in their double bed. Will her hand wake before her mind, will it creep, looking for her, across those purple sheets she bought from the thrift store last week? There's always a cinnamon smell to Ada, and tangles in her dyed red hair.

She should go back, get their breakfast made, kiss Ada awake. Shift this shade of melancholy into a brighter colour. In the moment they met, Ada's eyes danced, and all these years later, her glorious smile softens her line-ravaged face. At their wedding, Ada looked so gawky and relieved that she'd have grabbed her and kissed her carnivorous, right there, if they'd not been so closely watched by their families.

Melanie remembers the dead kittens she found in a cardboard box near the park one night and how she cried over them for days. Little black and white things, so tiny and so sad. Too small to yet be weaned. She remembers fairylights on festive pine trees, and how a tree being inside the house at all, let alone in a plant pot, felt like magic. She remembers waking up in a dentist's chair and seeing her favourite band spinning round in the air in front of her, singing out of tune. She remembers the deep ache in her jaw.

The star is still there, but a little fainter.

She whispers, "Why are these memories flooding, now?"

o oo o

It's all right. Everything is in the right place.

Last night Melanie couldn't sleep. She'd been up watching the news, and one mad president was threatening another mad president, but no one's brave enough to take either of them down. She wishes she was younger, wishes she could be an assassin, wishes she had a valid passport and no shortage of cash or disguises. The world would be a better place if certain people could…

disappear.

Is that what it's called, when a hit is made?

Melanie remembers her grandfather's memories of trenches and warfare. The smell of soil, socks, bad breath and stale teabags. She remembers his fear. She remembers her grandmother hoping and waiting and hoping he'd come home again. How can she remember these things, when she wasn't yet born? She remembers the smell of the antiseptic soap her grandmother was washing her hands with at the exact moment her grandad arrived back again. She remembers joy, sorrow, relief in her chest like a collision.

She remembers waiting. She's waiting, now, on this bench, next to this ocean, on this morning. But what for?

Melanie remembers the redness and warmth of a womb. The texture of wet rose petals, the smells of blood. She remembers her own childhood spent wondering who her father really was, looking at famous men on the telly, seeking resemblances and familiarity in the exact slope of their shoulders, the gaps between their teeth, the hairline. She remembers stabs of odd pain in her chest in the moment her mother told her she probably had half-brothers and half-sisters all over the whole country. She remembers yellow mugs filled with too-hot-too-sweet tea, and her mother's voice saying, "A lorry driver. Just passing through. I didn't know his name – we didn't talk."

She remembers how as a child she'd talk to daisies and the daisies would talk back in high-pitched voices which sounded like singing. She remembers the three sisters who lived up the road who were always dirty and everyone at school bullied them. She remembers rolling down a wheat field with them laughing, making tracks in tall crops.

The cargo boats are further away, crossing the ocean to somewhere else.

Above them, the star shines faintly.

So many holes in the world, which people fall through. It's so often the wrong people who disappear.

Melanie asks the ocean, "Why all these memory-floods? What's happening?"

The ocean doesn't reply.

A flock of gulls fly over her head, shrieking as if something is chasing them.

This is just a stupid feeling of dread she's got from watching the news. From hearing one mad president threatening another mad president. Babbling like spoilt children still demanding the nurse-milk of their nannies. Those who want power should *never* be given it.

Blackbirds – a silent group of them fly in a whirl overhead and disappear. Do blackbirds usually flock? What's wrong with the birds?

It can't be that there really is something terrible, about to happen.

She blinks and the star blinks.

Melanie remembers all the screens she's ever watched. Televisions, computers, phones, bus timetable screens. All the things she's seen which she would never have seen without screens. Haunting images. Mushroom clouds. That poor girl whose clothes were torn away, running along a street with terror in her face. A shadow of a ladder against a wall. Appalling repetitions: images of aeroplanes crashing into tall buildings and people, real people, jumping out of office windows and falling.

Never the impact. Just that terrible drop, on repeat.

As if Melanie could make everything disappear right here on this bench, looking at this dawn, she clutches her head as she says to the star, "I wish I didn't remember so much. I mean it. I'm too full."

The star goes dark, grows intensely bright, explodes, and disappears.

b   m   b

m   o   b

o   b   o

b   b   m

b   o   b   m

b   o   b   m

o   m   b   b   b

o   m   b

elanie f rgets her na e and everything she’s just re e ered, ne thing at a ti e.

First, the light f dawn disappears, as night returns and eats the day. The ench vanishes, and she falls t the gr und. The sky a ve her flickers like white n ise. Shapes f r , as i ages c e int f cus. The wh le sky is a TV screen. n it she watches pe ple rise fr their graves and cli tall uildings, s ashing wind ws t get inside. Tw aer planes fly ackwards, pulling their trails ack int the selves and cal ly c ntinue t reverse thr ugh the sky till they land n the runway and send all the passengers ack thr ugh rder c ntr l and t their h es. A girl is terrified and naked, ut there’s a flash f light and a   and a thud that see s t c e fr everywhere. She is war and cl thed. Televisi n screens and c puter screens and ph ne screens and us ti eta le screens all flicker thr ugh the sky. It links and g es lank.

She links, and a cluster f stars appear. She links again, and there's a full   n.

Her e ries shrink and the i ages f the c ntain h les the c l ur f lilac. I ages she re e ers have lilac gaps. What c l ur is her fr nt d r? Lilac. What c l ur are Ada's eyes? Lilac.

The   n is carrying a carg   f lilac-c l ured dust.

It dr ps it n the city. As the dust falls fr   the sky, c ating everything, there's a che ical scent in the air. She staggers as she walks h e, and when she l ks ar und, there are h les everywhere and these h les are getting igger. The h le in that wind w is pale with the full   n shining n it. The tear in that electricity wire which has ade all the lights g   ut. The h le in her hand ag, filled in with lilac.

If she c uld speak, she's certain s e f her w rds w uld ju le, r disappear. When there are h les, language ust st p aking sense. Nu   spreads. There's a d g arking ut she can't see it.

There are cr ps in the night sky, a wh le field f unharvested wheat, stretching fr   the h riz n upwards, verhead, ey nd. Placing her hands n the gr und, she rises t her feet. She has t get h e. She appr aches the ain r ad, and a full   n casts light n the gh sts f three sch l friends running al ng the r ad, gripping daisies in their hands, picking ff their petals, stealing their s ngs.

As she walks al ng the pave ent, a l rry drives past and she s iles up at the driver, wh d esn't see her. She can't re e er her ther's v ice. What did it s und like, was there anything i p rtant, which she said? H w terri le n t t re e er. There's a h le in her ind which is ther-shaped and it ustn't e all wed t gr w.

As she nears the t wn centre, she l ks up at the stars and her heart feels c ntented and c ntained. Her hands feel strangely clean, as if she's washed and salt-scru ed the in the cean.

She pauses eside a garden where tall sunfl wers are e racing each ther and i agines tw kings hugging, th wearing freshly laundered green shirts. ehind the sunfl wers is a wind w, with the curtain pen. The televisi n screen is fizzing with white n ise. She's glad she isn't aware f w rld events, and is relieved n ne f the screens w rk.

There are n lights n, th ugh, and there's an e pty plantp t utside n the steps, with a layer f dried pine needles clustering in the dirt. Perhaps n ne is in that uilding at all. She passes the railings f a park, where sticks are arranged in piles f r nfires, ut n thing is urning. She grips the railings. A c l ny f cats have ccupied the park, fifty f the . N , a hundred r re. All f the are lack and white.

As she walks ack t wards the street she lives in, t her s all flat, her s all edr , and single ed, she wishes there was s e ne there waiting f r her. S e ne she l ves. ut she can’t re e er ever l ving any ne, n t like that.

She’s een lucky in any ways, she kn ws this. N ne she kn ws has ever died, she’s never had a girlfriend, her heart has never een r ken. N ne has ever hurt her. There are just vague e ries f pe ple wh didn’t atter uch t her, and an a sence f passi n. She d esn’t kn w if she’s issed ut n anything, ecause there is n thing there t iss. She can’t even re e er ever lying t any ne. She w nders why she hasn’t.

ut n thing ad has ever happened t her r any ne she kn ws. She has never heard any h rri le pers nal st ries, ut ad things ight happen t ther pe ple she hasn’t yet talked t . ut n w she thinks a ut it, she can’t re e er ever really talking t any ne, and can’t think f a single na e f a genuine friend. As she c ntinues t walk, the pave ents l k like card ard. She puts her hand in the p cket f her c at which c ntains her keys and purse. She clenches her purse and listens t the s unds f c ins, ut d esn’t kn w what value they have.

There are n trees in this r ad, and n w she thinks a ut it, n trees left standing in the park where all the cats were either. There ust have een s e nce, as there are tree-stu ps left, ut she can’t re e er the eing cut d wn. Surely s e ne w uld have said s ething? ut wh w uld have said it?

She glances at the tall h uses up and d wn either side f the street, realising she kn ws n ne f her neigh urs. D es she kn w this t wn? It see s unfa iliar. The uildings are all ade f thin plastic, leached pale as if they've een washed up n s e each. If a gale rushed thr ugh, the wh le t wn w uld e l wn away.

Where is the gale which will l w everything away?

And where are the irds?

She appr aches a fr nt d r and inserts her key int a paper l ck. The l ck tears as the key turns.

The sky darkens, and n w she can't see anything. Pausing f r a ent ef re tearing thr ugh the d r, she l ks up at the lack sky. F r a ent there's the s und f a d g, panting, and the f tsteps f s e ne running al ng the pave ent. ut she can't see the , s can't elieve they're there.

Where are the irds?

She keeps staring int the darkness. There ust e a gale in the sky, as the n has een l wn away, and she'll iss it, th ugh she never thered with it that uch, she just n ticed it fr ti e t ti e.

ut… where are the irds?

LISP 2023 Flash Fiction Finalist

Kwame MA McPherson

I Wonder If They See Me

Rain pelts me, soaks my baseball cap. It drips droplets that slide from my poncho; pool at my feet. Holes are in my boots. Grey clouds match my mood. Under leafy trees we've been waiting for a while. In front of us, a swollen, roaring river. It's loud. We stare at it and toward the other bank.

I fix my rucksack. It's heavy. We'd been on the road for days and only the rising and falling sun informed me of the passing time since our watches were taken by the smugglers, long disappeared. We stand on the riverbank. It's a long wait.

A few men, women; like me. Young. Ambitious. Desperate. There's even one woman with a baby. I wonder how she'll manage the crossing since the promised raft is not where it's supposed to be or what we were told. Nobody says anything, every covered head slouches deep into shoulders. I'm scared. We're all afraid, wet and cold.

I wonder why I choose to be where I am? Why I left my home? My wife and children? I can see Maria. She's in the kitchen, cooking and crying. I'd told her it was to find a way to make our life better. A man must be a man, I say.

I feel my throat constrict. Some guy decides he can't wait and steps uncertainly into the raging water. I think he's crazy. He wades deeper, one shaky step at a time. I hold my breath; like everyone else, I'm sure. The rain tumults, clouds skid across the sky.

The water passes my ankles, reaches my knees and slaps my waist. My rucksack weighs heavier, pulls me down but I keep going. I stagger. I see my family - I wonder if they see me.

LISP 2023 Poetry Finalist
Ivy Raff

Prospect Park with My Mother During an Ectopic Pregnancy

/

She's traversed the Hudson:
unaccustomed juxtaposition.

When I'm well my complexities
scratch at her surface and she stays

in Jersey, longs for the tiny girl I was,
curls in 'tails, nose in books,

before I absconded to the loud side
of the river. Now the baby

must die so I can live. I didn't want to be a mother.
She wanted to be a grand/mother but not like this.

//

In these shadow-weeks, each
day may dawn my last. She's come

to witness the impending hemorrhage.
I'm sick, finally, and this she knows

how to get on with. No stories
from Rome or Taiwan, no book recommendations

to tax her scattered concentration, to remind her
she neither travels nor reads. Pregnant and dying,

eyes smoke and sunken, I look nothing
like the smack-talking kid she scolded after the rape,

It's the way you carry yourself.
He could smell it on you.

My mouth lacks the strength
for the twenty-year snarl I send her.

She simmers milk for my oatmeal,
shimmies my coat over my shoulders.

///

The doctors say walk,
but just a little. Blood must not pool,

must not rush. Orange gilds oaks,
particularly vibrant this year.

Red more rebellious. Every pace
a gift: felled-leaf fire curls

on concrete steps, the air's cool
with kisses. Every day we stroll

slow, so the dam won't burst.

LISP 2023 Short Story Finalist
Tunde Oyebode

Tenner

I'd spent the last of my money on a cheap navy suit and wore it to interviews. I hung it neatly underneath the skylight of the cold loft I rented.

There wasn't much to look at or do in the loft. It wasn't much bigger than the double bed I was sitting on.

At the edge of the bed, I was focused on the black-framed piece of paper hung on the opposite white wall: *Tamilore Ogunmakin, Master of Architecture with Distinction, July 2016*. It was March 2017. I'd been to fifteen interviews since then.

I began to feel cold and wore my sweatshirt. I didn't feel warmer, and a draught wafted through the skylight.

My belly ached. I was hungry. So I went down three floors to the kitchen of the four-storey Victorian corner house and toasted a slice of bread. While waiting for the toast, I noticed the name *Sara* written on the wrapping of the loaf, and then the toast popped up.

I ate the toast while leaning on the counter with my elbows and read the note stuck on the cupboard door. It hadn't been there the day before.

It read: *There is a thief in this house. Time after time, my food goes missing. Whoever you are, I don't share food. Please stop taking my food! It is annoying to come home late from work and not find what I'd left in the fridge. I'm not the only one that has this problem. Some other people in this house have complained too. So please, whoever you are, stop taking our food. Sara.*

I finished the toast and put another slice of bread in the toaster. Butter and jam on toast had never tasted so wonderful.

After I showered, I sprayed my suit with Febreze and then put it on with a pair of black brogues with wonky soles. I laid my bed, pulling the covers tight and tucked it underneath the mattress, then fluffed the single pillow I had.

I picked up my folder, which was leaning against the wall and checked it for my CV and portfolio. They were both there. I sat on my bed, leafing carefully through the pages I had bound. I stopped at a drawing and photograph of a prototype model of one of my projects, a community school in East Africa.

I looked up at the certificate, then myself in the mirror underneath. I smiled. There wasn't much to be happy about. But my Afro was perfectly rounded.

I closed the portfolio and zipped the folder, then brushed my hand across the bed to remove the creases. I looked around to make sure everything was in place—neat—and headed out.

It was after nine a.m. London was cold and noisy. I folded my arms and tucked my hands underneath my armpits. The interview for an architectural assistant was at 11 a.m. in southwest London, five miles away. I checked my pockets for change. I was down to my last tenner. I decided to walk.

I arrived in good time and waited at a bus stop a hundred metres away from the office to practise my lines, reading from my notes. 'Why do you think you're perfect for this role? I'm thorough, creative and keen to challenge myself.' I recited the lines over and over. 'I'm imaginative, ambitious and detail-oriented.' The bus stop became crowded. I put the notes in my breast pocket and headed to the office.

—

The office was warm and smelt of coffee. The receptionist, a tall skinny man with long blonde hair and a pair of round clear-framed glasses, offered me a drink.

'I'm imaginative, ambitious and creative.' Still practising the lines. I sat waiting for my interviewers with a glass of water cupped between my palms.

I'd not paid last month's rent, and if I'd not threatened to report my landlord for illegally renting the tiny loft space to me I would've been kicked out.

The shelves on the bookcase opposite were filled with samples: bricks, tiles and glass. They were shoved into whatever space was available. Some were left on the floor. The adjacent bookcase wasn't any tidier. Behind me was a window that overlooked the studio. It had a long central table with computers backing each other. Everyone looked busy—papers everywhere.

The glass door slid open, and I stood to greet the woman and man who entered. As I shook their hands, I caught a glimpse of myself in the mirror on the adjacent wall. Somehow, on the walk to the interview, my Afro had lost its roundness, marred with lumps and valleys. It was too late for a comb, so I put on my best smile.

The woman was short, fiery-haired and quick with her words. When she spoke, I paid attention. The man was tall with long fingers. He tapped the table as he listened. His intense gaze made me feel cold, yet I was sweating. I'd been to numerous interviews but could never shake the fear that nothing would come of it. I fingered my moustache and the stubble on my chin while speaking, aware my face was wet with perspiration.

The words I'd practised came out disjointed. And as he continued to stare, my speech dwindled. Nothing I said made sense. I mumbled.

The fiery-haired lady stopped me, took my portfolio, and skimmed through it. The man continued to stare at me with half a smile on his face. He'd said nothing. As she flipped the pages—the papers made splitting sounds. I'd bound the portfolio by sewing each piece of paper together and glueing a hardcover to keep it all in place. She stopped flipping the pages and said, 'Why did you apply for this job?'

The question irritated me. I'd been to several interviews. Architecture jobs are competitive. Because of this, I had to apply to jobs that required fewer qualifications—all with the same result. Wasn't it clear?

'Um…well, actually, I applied after seeing your homeless shelter project in South London. The warm and tactile materials gave the space a domestic feel. It's community architecture that feels homely, beautiful and safe. I'm interested in architecture for the community, for the everyday person.'

The fiery-haired lady smiled. 'That was a one-off project. We often do projects for private clients: high-end stuff. We were lucky that the council paid us enough to break even.' She turned the pages to the drawing of the school in East Africa. I'd designed the building to be self-built by the everyday person with mud and timber.

'These aren't the skills we're looking for,' the slender-fingered man finally said, looking at my portfolio. 'We're interested in highly skilled work.'

Photos of various projects by the firm hung on the wall. They were Victorian house extensions and pristine contemporary houses with colourful tiles and neat bricks.

'I think my skills are transfer…'

'We need someone with interest in the type of architecture we do,' he said.

I was sweating even more now. My suit felt tight. I was tense and desperate.

'I need the job for rent, food, clothes, and to have a life,' I said pleadingly.

The fiery-haired lady closed the portfolio and looked at me. Silence. They were both expressionless. Then she said, 'we have other interviews today, actually one in five minutes. And others lined up this week. We will contact you by the end of this week if you are successful.'

I knew I'd lost the job. How would I get out of paying rent for another month? I could threaten the landlord again. Or I could promise more, as long as he let me stay one more week to find a job. Any job. I'd been a cleaner while studying. I spent my free afternoons in the houses of West London families. I was good. They asked me back many times, and some families employed me to organise their wardrobes.

'I didn't mention,' I said as the interviewers rose. They both looked puzzled. 'Actually,' I pulled out my CV from the folder. 'Here,' I pointed to the column with work experience. 'I spent a lot of my free time tidying and cleaning homes in west London while studying. I can clean and tidy the studio,' I said and looked around the room.

The fiery-haired woman smiled and nodded thoughtfully, then held out her hand. I stood and shook her extended hand. 'Thanks for listening to me. Thanks for the opportunity.' I shook the man's hand. His fingers were just as chilly as his gaze. I picked up my folder and my portfolio and then left the office.

—

It was lunchtime. I walked two miles to meet Matt at an Art Deco Café on King's Road, close to his work. We went to university together. He worked for a prestigious architectural firm with a glass building overlooking the River Thames in southwest London.

He looked good, with a fresh-out-of-the-shop haircut. His hands were warm as he shook mine and smiled.

'How you doing, boy? It's been long?'

It was sunny now. We decided to sit outside under the glass canopy overlooking the traffic on King's Road.

'I'm good,' I said.

'So what you been up to?' he said.

'Just been to an interview.'

'Yeah, how'd it go?'

'Well. Think I am going to get it,' I said, smiling.

He smiled his usual smile; eyes squinted, the lines around his mouth stretched almost to his temples. His hairline, which had already started to recede, moved with his smile and pushed back further, accentuating the size of his forehead. It gave him a sinister look. I was younger than him, but he looked much older.

'Nice one, boy. Nice one,' he said.

He hardly referred to me by name—always boy, bro, dude or something like that—mostly boy. We've known each other for three years. You'd think he would've learnt how to say TAMILORE.

'So what did your boss say?' I said.

He'd stopped smiling and was looking behind me. His latte arrived. The waiter asked me if I was sure I didn't want anything.

'I'm fine, thank you,' I said, thinking about my tenner. She smiled and left.

'She's pretty hot, isn't she?' Matt said, returning his gaze to me after watching the waitress walk away.

'I guess so.'

Two blonde women walked past us, and he looked them over.

'So what did your boss say? You think I have a chance?' I said.

'She saw your portfolio,' he said.

'And?'

'She seemed to like it. But she didn't say much else.'

'You reckon I could get her email?'

'Not sure.'

'Why not?'

He didn't say anything.

'Well, why not?'

'Last week, some geezer was standing at the front door with his portfolio on boards and easels. He'd been emailing the boss every week before then…'

'I'm not gonna do that shit,' I interrupted.

'Okay… I'll ask her. Don't worry. Leave it to me.'

How had he secured his job so quickly? He wasn't great at university.

'Do you remember Lauren?' he asked as he lifted his right hand to his face. He twisted the gold signet ring on his pinkie with his thumb.

'Yeah. Why?' I asked.

'She called me yesterday,' he said, smiling.

'What did she want?' I said.

'Obviously to talk to me,' he said, laughed, and sipped his latte.

'I thought she hates your guts,' I said.

'Well, I guess she's forgiven me. I guess she's lonely and realised how much of a catch I am.' His right hand was on the table now. He continued twisting the ring. The act gave his hand an odd deformity as if he'd lost his thumb.

'She asked to meet me,' he said.

Lauren was a friend from university. I liked her a lot and wanted to be more than friends, but she dated Matt instead. He cheated. I never heard from her again.

'So what you going to do?' I asked.

'What else, boy? I'm going to meet up and bring her back home,' he said, focusing his gaze on his pinkie. He'd stopped twisting the ring with his thumb, and his hand lay flat on the timber table—fingers splayed. I wondered if anyone could draw without a thumb.

'Okay,' I said.

He looked at me. 'What's wrong?' he asked.

I said nothing, just turned my gaze to the building and stared at the large white crest on the fascia of the building's roof.

'What?' he asked.

I looked at him. 'I just think…nothing, don't worry about it.'

'Jesus Christ, she called me. I didn't call her.'

'Look, it's your business. You can do whatever you want,' I said. We were silent for a moment. The traffic on King's Road became noticeable. How did he have everything?

'Don't you have to get back to work?' I asked.

He looked at his watch and finished the rest of his latte.

'Maybe something might come of it. We can get back together,' he said. 'I'm sorry for what I did, you know.'

He stood up and put on his jacket.

'I'd prefer something come of my CV you gave to your boss. Let me have her email.'

'Don't worry. I got you. I'll speak to her again. Soon boy. Soon.'

—

I had nothing left to do for the afternoon, so I decided to go home, apply for more jobs and practise for interviews. I'd done enough walking for the day, so I walked to the nearest tube station, Sloane Square. It was sunnier—people in sunglasses, low-cut tops, t-shirts and no jackets. Any sign of the sun, and they were at it like it was full-blown summer. But it would only last a minute.

I got to the station and reached into my trouser pocket to get my tenner. I checked my breast pocket, the inner pocket of my jacket and my back pockets. 'Where had I lost it?' I began mentally retracing my steps. Confused and frustrated.

I was standing in the middle of the station when a man wearing a large backpack approached me. He was upset and confused.

'Shepherd's Bush?'

I couldn't decipher his accent. 'Sorry, what?'

'Shepherd's Bush!' People stared as the man shouted *Shepherd's Bush* over and over again.

I tried to describe the route with hand gestures and words. He nodded but looked at me blankly when I stopped. I walked him to the underground map, retrieved a pen from my breast pocket, and began drawing on the back of a page of my portfolio. It was the back of the self-built school. It was coming off the binding. I drew out the route to Shepherd's Bush with the significant changeover stations only. Sloane Square, yellow line, then Notting Hill Gate, red line, finally Shepherd's Bush. I drew over it again, making it bold. He looked at me eagerly and in distress, and then I tore the paper neatly from the portfolio and handed it to him. He studied it for a few seconds, then looked at me, smiled, and said thank you.

After he'd gone, I took out my oyster card, hoping there was money on it. To my surprise, I had 5.90, enough to get home. All I wanted was to get home. So I tapped in and walked through the barrier.

The tube was about to leave. I ran, nearly getting caught by the closing doors. I sat, catching my breath. There were many people. We were all trying to get somewhere. Sat opposite me was the man wearing the large backpack. He smiled and said thank you several times. All that was on my mind was the tenner I'd lost. I wondered if everyone else was thinking about money. The train approached Notting Hill Gate, and I indicated to the man that his stop was next. He nodded, stood up, said thank you and reached into his pocket for something. He stuck his hand out to shake me, and in his hand was a tenner.

'Oh no. No need for that,' I said, standing up, closing the gap between us to hide the money.

He shook his head and forced the money back into my hand. Everyone in the carriage stared at us. I caught a glimpse of my reflection in the window behind the man. Embarrassed, I stopped looking at myself and looked at the man. He was smiling—the tenner clasped between our hands.

'Take, thank you,' he said and hurried out of the carriage just before the doors closed. I sat back in my seat and looked around the carriage with the tenner in my hand. People stared. I put the money in the right front pocket of my trousers. While doing so, I felt a tiny slit in the lining. I put my fingers in it and found a piece of paper. It was the tenner I thought I'd lost. I folded both tenners and put them into another pocket.

What food could I buy at the shop? How long could I make it last? Then I got a pen out of my pocket, ripped out the rest of the torn page in my portfolio and wrote a note: *I'm not a thief. I'm hungry and desperate. I've had no work.* I looked at the note for a while as the train rattled on and crossed out: ~~*I'm hungry and desperate*~~. Then crossed out: ~~*I've had no work*~~. It still didn't feel right, so I wrote a list of what to buy at the shops and considered replacing Sara's loaf.

End

LISP 2023 Flash Fiction Finalist
Sue Harper

Dancing

She was driving him home on the night of the full moon. She turned into the churchyard - all the sleepers were still - and parked, stilled the engine. The earth seemed to be breathing. They got out of the car and turned to look at each other. He switched the car radio on, and the music came flooding out. They circled round each other in perfect harmony, their movements echoing each other's. They put their arms round each other, her hand on his shoulder, his arm round her waist. And there amongst the gravestones, they began to dance together.

How it happened she was never sure, but they began to float. First an inch or two off the dusty ground, then a foot or two, then they were swirling slowly above the treetops and the houses. He was looking at her at last. Heaven can be another person, she thought. An owl flapped by them, and someone seemed to be playing a violin. Its tune made them soar upwards.

And that was how love came at last. No gravity, but a searing sweetness. The night was deep blue. She hoped that the morning would not come. And for them, it never did.

LISP 2023 Poetry Finalist
Alison Grove

Photo Taken On A Dappled Day

The occasion calls for a rare solo spot

Mumbling a priestly spell
he nimbly dealt each offered tongue
a sacred Tarot card,
a Patience playing grandma
pressing fate into our mouths.

and I look pleased with the elbow room.

I hoped there'd be a holy jolt -
miraculous heat, Good News.
Colleen Fahy – ribboned and flounced,
meringued down to her white patent toes,
silver Communion bracelet
a slithering coveted gleam –
breathed an incense curl:
Did you feel it? Did you feel the *power*?

Dutifully dappling, the apple tree

Rapture sparked like nylon
but I couldn’t say I had.
Sin-smudged in knee-high
Crimplene deep-hemmed against
my future Confirmation, I watched
my school shoes shrugging off
their painted coats.

is working on her maggoty crop

It left me like a sudden moult,
a fall of leaves,
joyous as a slip of silk.
I took to patent heels
bracelets to the elbow
the complex coil of Mortal Sin.

sifting sunlight into marbled shade.

LISP 2023 Short Story Finalist
Gina Challen

Nuisance Calls

She travels for miles. It's what she does, striding out across the chalk hills in the company of her dogs, the two animals as sleek-coated and lithe as she is scruffy and dumpy. She tramps on paths where, over time, footsteps and rain have flayed the topsoil away until all that is left is flint-embedded chalk, exposed like ancient bones.

Up here, she catches the acrid musk of a fox, or spots the flash of deer as they spring away from her intrusion. In truth, she is the outsider in this world and she tries to make her passing as fleeting and unobtrusive as she can. It's different for the dogs, they belong, generation after generation, tied by their lupine ancestors to the land.

The dogs run on ahead. The older, steady male is a path-finder, always checking over his shoulder to make sure she is following, whilst the little bitch, young, flighty and highly strung, hunts through the undergrowth for mice and voles. This youngster is tricky, her character not yet fully formed and neither dog nor human are used to her ways of being. Ancient, twisted yews stand between rows of much younger, straighter plantings.

These trees are her waymarkers, and she takes comfort in their presence as she moves through the woods.

Right now, the country is in the grip of a heatwave and, leaving her partner in bed, she brings the dogs out early to avoid the worst of it. Even so, as she leans across to kiss Liz goodbye, she worries. There have been days of clear blue skies and temperatures soaring into the nineties by lunchtime. Venture outside and the sun pricks hard against bare flesh. Most feel a slick of sweat around the hairline. In the afternoons, the heat pushes down and a torpor settles over the countryside. The lucky ones keep indoors with their curtains drawn tight. Water levels have dropped, gardens are parched and the shops sell out of ice cream. The media have a field-day, filling up with stories of the foolhardy. Take care, they warn. Look after the young and the elderly. Some people love it, some hate it and everybody she speaks to has a story to tell.

On the hills, the paths are baked solid and each step kicks up a dust to coat her trainers. Later, at home, there will be an anklet of dirt encircling her flesh when she pulls off her socks. In places the air is filthy with flies. Tiny and black, they hang in clouds and, hand on the peak of her cap, she hurries through. All along the tracks, the nettles and brambles have grown high and straggly. Filling the fence lines, the white flower heads of the cow parsley are as faded and grubby as old, net curtains. The heavy air gathers into pockets, hot and overloaded with the stench of scat. Already, the day feels musty and used and she tastes the staleness of it at the back of her throat.

Following the track, she emerges from the shade of the trees into the full force of the sun. Quickly, she shuts her eyes against the glare and, for the moment they are closed, shapes flick and dance behind her eyelids. Her thoughts are skittish, full of scrappy half-sentences, of words that, sometime soon, will need to be spoken. Nothing is fully formed or tangible, and she is a bother to herself. Try as she might, it's difficult to know when things began to be different with her mother. When they'd asked her at the hospital, the doctor brisk and efficient, his next crisis waiting, she couldn't say. Later, sitting with Liz on hard plastic chairs beside the bed, she took her mother's hand and wondered aloud if it had been a gradual shift. In the dimmed light of the night time ward, she wonders if it was something she should have spotted.

When she rounds the edge of the meadow, there is no sign of either dog on the open sweep of rabbit-bitten grass. Until recently, this area of chalkland was barely enclosed, the boundaries marked only by rotten posts and broken strands of rusting wire. Crops replaced the grass with acid-yellow rape and tangles of bright, green peas. These days, all is different. Labourers have been at work replacing posts, stretching out stock fencing and capturing the Down between the taut lines of galvanised steel. White and purple clover, pink vetch and rich, gold buttercups are scattered across the ground. The land has been returned to itself. Come the spring, she has been told, sheep and cattle will be brought up to graze and all will change once more.

Where this part of the Downs ends, there's a crease in the bedrock and the fold of chalk broadens out, quietly rising to the shoulder of the next hill. This margin is thicketed with hawthorn and tangled brambles, together forming a dense hedgerow. She aims for a small clearing, a bite of land between the footpath and the thicket. This is where she finds the dogs, their tails high, snuffling amongst the shrub. An old shepherds' hut once stood here casting an early morning shadow across the ground, but it has been taken, uprooted by the owner, and all that is left is the dappled shade of the hawthorn and a log for a bench. She sits. Taking a bottle and a bowl from her bag, she pours water for the dogs.

Last Saturday, there had been an incident. Another fall. A day spent in A & E and a night in a chair beside a hospital bed. Another day disrupted and lost that shouldn't have been so.

Another day in ruins. Thinking of it, drains her, yet she cannot stop these lost hours spooling through her thoughts in crushing sequences. How quickly the day had turned, from her own, to her mother's. The moment the old woman had slumped to the floor, her head bumping the tiles, the day had flipped, faster than a tossed coin.

The Down at her back, she gazes across the curve of the pasture cloaking the next hill. Please say, this is not her fault. As Liz has told her, she can't be there all the time. She visits, takes her mother shopping and does the heavy cleaning. More than this, she phones twice a day. In the mornings, she calls around 7.45am because her mother takes her tablets and eats her breakfast at 8.00am. In the afternoons, she calls around 4.45pm because her mother always cooks dinner at 5.00.

Even here in the shade, the heat is beginning to build, pricking across her arms and the back of her neck. The dogs watch her. The male, panting, tongue out, sits close, his head resting on her leg, and she feels the warmth from his body and the swift beat of his heart. True to herself, the little bitch lies in the cool of the long grass, with them, yet apart from them.

Sometimes, usually in the afternoon, she gets the timing wrong and her call interrupts the preparation of her mother's evening meal.

'Carry on, I am listening to you,' her mother says, but the tone is terse and the call is cut short. In the background, she hears the clatter of saucepans or the gush of water from a tap as the old woman continues with her cooking, and she knows, beyond any doubt, she has misjudged once again. She is a nuisance. She has always been a nuisance and, no matter how often it happens, or how she readies herself, the old woman's snub is as fierce and spiteful as the sting from a wasp.

The dogs have settled beside the seat and are flat out, prone in the shadows, half-asleep. As she watches the slow rise and fall of their rib cages, her head swarms with slights and rebuffs, with conversations that need to be had and words waiting to be spoken. All her life it has been so. This constant conflict between them. Her striving for approval, for a tender word, for unconditional praise, pitted against her mother's wants and needs, likes and dislikes.

Around her, under a bright, clear sky, the morning unwinds. She watches a blackbird pause, head tilted, as it scans the dry, solid earth for a meal. Unlucky, it runs forward, then stops to search again. When she was eight, she'd run away. She'd packed her pyjamas, a book and a jumper in her school bag, emptied her piggy bank and left. A small, dark-haired girl hurrying through the twittens that led between the houses. Ten years later, she left again, but, somehow, she's never been able to go very far. In the grass by the log, the old dog snores, gentle sounds that cause his ears to twitch. She leans down, runs her hand across the soft dome of his head, and he stills.

Yesterday, when the doctor spoke with her, his words had been kind, but his intent had been firm and his meaning, clear. Her mother is deteriorating, each fall leaving her weaker than the last. She glances back to the blackbird working its way deeper under the hawthorn. Her sleep over, the little bitch becomes restless and investigates the water bowl. She takes a couple of laps then turns her attention once more to snuffling in the scrub. With a sudden swiftness, the young dog darts forward, her muzzle thrust amongst the brambles, the plume of her tail high. Prick-eared and bright eyed, the bitch straightens, a kill clamped tightly in her mouth.

This last year, she has felt that all the things her mother doesn't like or want are slowly seeping into her world. Each one close on the heels of another, problem upon problem, bleeding into the world she shares with Liz. Their life has become a litany of all her mother's issues. It would be easier if there was some common view-point between herself and her mother, one beyond their maternal and filial relationship. If only she could see a shared understanding, a compassion or empathy that could hold them closer than their blood.

No matter what, my daughter will look after me, her mother has told the nursing staff. This has a frightening certainty.

Surely, her mother can't believe that will happen. She can't expect such a thing. It's too much to ask of anyone. Her mother can't expect such a thing, not from someone who's always been a nuisance. She looks towards the dogs, the male is still dozing and the bitch is fidgeting, the dead mouse at her feet, ready to leave. They should go home before it becomes any hotter. She must get up, dust herself off and retrace her steps. As Liz has told her, there's no point in keep looking back and raking through the hurt.

Rising, she gathers up the water bowl, flicking the remaining liquid out into the sunlight and seeing the droplets shatter as they hit the hard-packed earth. Shouldering the bag, she arches her back to ease her aching muscles. The young bitch, glad they are moving at last, picks up the mouse and moves away from the undergrowth. The male dog stands. He stretches and shakes his head. *My daughter will look after me.* The words terrify her. As she steps onto the track, the relentless heat hits her and she pulls at the peak of her cap to shield her face.

She's glad to reach the cool of the woods, glad to bring the dogs away from the sun's glare and into the shade. It's always quicker going home. Of course, it isn't, yet, walking amongst the trees, the paths between the waymarkers seem shorter and she smiles when she spots the first yew, the mound of its dark, green foliage sharp against the blue sky. She stops to rest when she reaches it and, leaning against the trunk, feels the rough, cool, peel of the bark through her shirt. The dogs mill around her legs, eager to carry on.

Dropped or eaten, the young bitch has lost her kill, and she moves with ease, slipping from shadow to shadow at the edge of the track. They have not gone far when a breeze picks up and catches across the flat-branches of the beeches. The leaves above her begin to rustle, the sound quickening until she can hear it in all directions like the wash of an incoming tide. It brings with it the taste of rain yet there are no clouds and, before she can wonder if the weather is breaking, the breeze dies down as if it has never been.

Thick and dry, pine needles shift underfoot. She's cutting back through the edge of the fir plantings, when the sudden, raucous cries of angry rooks shatter the silence and startle her. The birds erupt from the trees, screaming and jostling for space as they crowd, black-winged, into the sky. Their calls are loud and argumentative, and the sound of their quarrelling fills the spaces around her. Unexpectedly, words begin to join together in her head. Sentences begin to form into the conversations she must have. Above her, high in the canopy, the rooks, their disagreement done, settle back, for now, in their roost. She calls to the dogs: her stride lengthens and she picks up speed. Out in front, the dogs begin to run.

LISP 2023 Flash Fiction Finalist
Laurie Bolger

Big Drop

I like to begin my day with 100 cups of coffee
and I like to end it sitting in a chair with a beer
or against my big pillows and just sip
            kick back as they say
and I don't think it's the feeling of getting drunk or anything
like that
I think it's that first sip   it does something
like when you open the cold fridge after a long shift
            kick off your shoes
                        flip the red lid
push the glass circle to your lips and let it get stuck there as you
sup the first fizz and go *ahhhhh* —
I used to watch this kids programme with a postman called Pat
he had this cat called Jess
and after a hard day he'd twist the lid off of a glass bottle
                        and just neck it
I've always been obsessed with watching men down things
            being called *one of the lads* and not being allowed to
go to the stag

I remember sitting on the back step listening for them
left in with pinks straws and glitter
I listened for their chanting
the first time I got properly drunk a boy carried me to the car
like some sort of damsel
                    I was light enough to be lifted up
                                                  like catch of the day
once I got so drunk I hit a man's chest hard
            with my fists
I felt wild —

LISP 2023 Poetry Finalist
Hannah Stephings

Sentimental Garbage

I hope you keep finding my hair
six months after we break up
strands of my DNA still messing up the exposed faux-oak floor
of your bedroom
snagged into the pages of 'Zen and the Art of Motorcycle
Maintenance' which you lent me in an attempt to impress
and I let you feel like a tiny god, explaining it over Greek
takeaway.

Spider-fragile reminders, matted little tumbleweeds that
nestle behind closed doors, in hidden, intimate corners,
skittering into your day unexpected and infuriating.

Collateral forget-me-nots, clogging up the shower, enmeshed
in your mattress-topper, coiled in wait under sofa cushions,
stubborn 'I-was-here's
despite your insistence we were never anything to get hung up
about.

You'll get backache untangling my snarled presence from the hoover's jaws
and I'll tell you I'm sorry for the inconvenience,
with my fingers crossed.

LISP 2023 Flash Fiction Finalist
Linda Jorgenson

Cold Beer

I'm sweat'n like bacon fry'n on the cooker. Bloody hell, open the windows.

So, I did, didn't I? I unlocked 'em and swung 'em out as far as they'd go– all of 'em, even the ones to the patio. Still, she wasn't happy.

Get the fan down from the loft.

So, I did that too.

Bring me a cold beer from the fridge.

I placed the bottle right next to her as she flicked through the channels.

Hey. Get me a glass.

Her eyes fixed on Ken Barlow in *Coronation Street*. The omnibus edition.

I set down her favourite thick tumbler, and said, *I'm go'in for a walk.*

When I got back the front door gaped like an entrance to a cave. Two police officers stood over the body. A neighbour'd called 'em. Said they'd heard a woman scream'n.

The volume was still up. Ken Barlow wore a short-sleeved, plaid, shirt. He was cry'n. One of his wives was dead.

My one and only lay in a pool of blood. The red was start'n to turn the carpet brown.

Condensation slithered down the beer bottle.

She hadn't even touched it.

LISP 2023 Poetry Finalist
Fiona Dignan

Relic

Of course, I'm still fourteen years away
from the rock you stand on. Barefoot
seafoam like lace against your bronzed legs
Your hands all your own
like your name and the pink towel dress which licks
your thighs. Always a *yes* in your mouth
back then. The faceless American boy exists

behind the lens, a man who will seal you
in monochrome but not become my father. He will hang
as an absence like all those things
from our personal histories
we cannot know. Just a Yankee twang
telling you to pose. I have to imagine

the colours of that St Ives summer, the whitewash
of the hotel you worked in, the sapphire
of the ocean expanse and the gold fizz

of the stars you and Aunty Carol call to
in your giddy state. Imagining too the sounds

of those iconic boy-gods who pluck
at guitars in the beachy night air
the scent of smoke soaking their cotton shirts. We all play
at things in youth, as though the notes
will eventually right themselves. How could you know

back then, amongst the salmon sunsets, the nights
were imperceptibly closing in and one day
you would need to count all those small deaths
There must have been seconds
when the photo was a blank white page, before

your image comes into being and your presence becomes
a certainty impressed into the future

Your pink towel dress hangs in my closet
now, in a suburban semi but I pretend
I can still smell that summer on it, smoke and possibility
when my children and I were still tucked
inside you like Russian dolls

not yet imagined as the two stripes of pink

positives, becoming a presence on the blank white test

LISP 2023 Flash Fiction Finalist
Niles Reddick

A Drunk Cedar Waxwing

The bird flew right into the front glass door, and we heard a thump. I figured it was neighborhood boys who'd thrown a ball at the house again. "By mistake," they'd squawked. The bird tried to move its wings but couldn't take flight. "What kind of bird is it?" I asked.

Robin said, "It's a Cedar Waxwing. Must be flying drunk." She opened the door, squatted, and took it gently in her hands.

"Drunk? I have heard of pilots flying drunk but not a bird."

"It's okay, pretty girl.' She cooed. She stood and held the bird. "They eat fermented berries whole and often get drunk. Usually, they are in a flock, not alone."

I remember a chimney swift bird getting into Nana's house when I was a teen. It had been startled, and because the chimney flue was open, it flew inside instead of out. Nana shrieked as if it were a mouse in her pantry or a snake in her lilies, and while she limped and hid behind the door to the kitchen, she directed me to open the back door to the patio, to get the broom to scare and guide it outside without hitting it. The sooty gray bird flew out and within weeks, I could hear her babies screeching in the chimney.

With a few head shakes and flapping of its wings, the Cedar Waxwing took off, and I told Robin she should wash her hands.

LISP 2023 Short Story Finalist
Tina Pisco

Madame Marieke

Madame Marieke sat on the bed as she waited for the milk to heat on the little hob in the back room. She rummaged around in her corset until her fingers caught, and then pulled out two crisp fifties and a crumpled twenty. She lay them out side by side, smoothing them flat as if she were ironing them, before gathering them up and popping them into her purse. One more client and she'd call it a night. Her hip was acting up, and she still had to walk Lola.

Madame Marieke checked the milk by putting a drop on her wrist, a trick she had learnt when Cecile was a baby. She didn't often think about her daughter, but this was one of those times. Madame Marieke switched on the radio to chase the memory away before it turned into something sad and heavy. The milk was perfect, just a bit warmer than blood temperature. She poured a bit of the hot liquid into her favourite blue mug and mixed it with two heaped teaspoons of cacao and one of sugar until she had a smooth paste. She then poured the rest of the milk in slowly, stirring as she hummed along to a song that had been popular when she was a schoolgirl.

Madame Marieke put the mug on a tray and gave herself two *gaufrettes* from the tin on the counter. She made a batch of the small waffles every Sunday evening as she watched television. The store-bought ones weren't as good. She opened the little fridge, took out a spray can and put a teetering crown of *Chantilly* on her hot chocolate. In her profession there was always some on hand. She'd never really understood it, but a lot of men had a thing about whipped cream.

The narrow room was predominantly red, from the ruby glow of the bulb in the pink tasselled lampshade of the ceiling light, to the cherry chenille bedspread. Madame Marieke prided herself in keeping the place clean and tidy. A single bed, a chair, and a closet took up most of the space. At the foot of the bed a swivel armchair and a small brass side table were framed by a bay window. Hung around the window frame were the tools of her trade: kinky boots in a size 45, dog collars, feather ticklers and fancy nipple clamps. These days she did more business tying men up and humiliating than fucking them, which suited her just fine. At her age she wasn't going to be doing anything too energetic. Thankfully, most of her clients were older men who needed help jerking off, or those who wanted to be told that they were very, very, bad boys.

Madame Marieke threw a scarlet boa around her neck, drew the curtains open, and arranged herself on her swivel armchair. The street was still fairly empty. It was the slow period between the quickie-after-work crowd, and the out-for-the-night crowd. Men passed up and down the street; some in twos or threes, but mostly alone. Men who had nothing better to do than to stroll the flashing neon streets of the red-light district; eating a burger from the McDonalds at the *Gare du Nord* train station, or a paper wrapped portion of fries from the *frite-kot* on the boulevard. Men who were delaying going home. Men who had no real home to go to, or whose homes were far away. Men in overalls. Men in suits. Many wore scarves, gloves, and big puffy jackets to ward off the wind. The *stomme* wind, as her father liked to call it, quoting the old Jacques Brel song she'd been named after. *Zonder liefde, warme liefde, Waait de wind, de stomme wind*. The stupid wind. The one that blows when there's no love, no *warme* love. Just cold, stupid wind.

If it started raining, she might as well go home early before the streets flooded, or worse, iced over. The seasons made no sense anymore. Last summer had been sweltering heatwaves and fires, while the spring had been the coldest she could remember. She promised herself to call an Uber if the rain got bad. Lola would have to be satisfied with a quick bathroom break in the courtyard. As the first raindrops splattered the pane, the thought of taking off her corset and curling up in her dressing gown with Lola was very appealing.

She didn't notice him at first. He stood very close to the corner of the window, his nose almost pressed to the glass, his ebony face bathed in red neon. His dark hoodie was pulled tight over his chin and forehead. His hands were shoved into the pockets. He was tall; six feet at least, but slight and willowy, with long arms and legs. His features were delicately pretty, even beautiful, with big doe eyes and bones like a little bird. This could be a very easy 50 euro, she thought.

He sat on the edge of the bed, his eyes wide, as he looked around the room. Madame Marieke closed the curtains, sat down on her swivel chair and turned to face him.

"*Tu parle Francais? Spreek je Vlaams*? Speak English?" she asked, crossing her legs and flashing her red lacy knickers.

He did not seem to hear her. In fact, he wasn't looking at her at all. Though his face was a picture of longing and his whole body trembled with desire, his eyes never left the blue mug sitting on the little side table. The cream had started to melt down the side. Madame Marieke picked up the mug and handed it to him. He took it and drained it in one long gulp.

"I am learning English. I am going to England," he said, still looking at the little table. Marieke reached over and handed him the two *gaufrettes*, which he accepted silently, and ate in quick bites.

"You can call me Madame Marieke. It's 50 euro for 20 minutes...."

He hung his head and closed his eyes, swaying slightly as if he was finding it hard to stay awake. "No money," he said. "The police chased us from the park. My bag is gone."

What was this now? She had seen the hundreds of people camping in the nearby *Parc Maximillian* but had not really taken any notice. They were like the beggars in the *Metro* with their strange sleeping children, or the pedlars that popped up anytime you sat down at a café terrace to have a quiet coffee and cake. She'd never really wondered who they were, or where they came from. This one was African. He was also very young. Fourteen, maybe fifteen at the most. Young and cold, and hungry.

"Did you eat today?" she asked, sitting back, and lighting a cigarette.

"Yesterday. From the volunteers in the park."

Madame Marieke took a long drag on her cigarette and shook her head; tut-tutting as she exhaled. "I have some left-over *boulettes.* Meatballs I made. Do you eat pork? The meatballs have pork in them."

"I am a Christian," he said, fishing out a chain and showing her a small crucifix, which he kissed before tucking it back inside his hoodie.

"So am I. Not that it's done me any good!" she said with a laugh. "Wait there. I'll be right back." Madame Marieke grabbed her housecoat off the back of the door and put it on as she slipped behind the beaded curtain into the back room. She unhooked her corset, and exchanged her red stilettos for soft, comfy slippers. She got the tin of *gaufrettes*, and gave it to him through the beads. "Eat these while I heat up the *boulettes.*"

He had eaten half the tin by the time she came back with a plate of three fragrant meatballs in a rich tomato sauce. She stood waiting as the boy closed his eyes, made the sign of the cross and held his hands in prayer. After a few short words, he looked up.

"We pray before eating," he explained. "I pray with my family. My mother is praying all day."

"What do you pray for," asked Madame Marieke.

"Rain. We pray for rain," he said, "and peace."

She gently took the tin from his lap and replaced it with the steaming plate. "It would be better with some *frites*, but it's too wet to run out and get some. We don't need to pray for rain here!" she said brightly, "I can bring more food from home in the morning. You can sleep here tonight, if you have nowhere else to go." she added, surprising herself as she said it.

He picked up the fork and speared a meatball, blowing on it to cool it down. "Thank you. You are very kind."

Madame Marieke sat smoking and watched him eat. When he had finished, she made him lie down on the bed, took off his shoes and covered him with the red chenille bed spread. He lay very still, his big doe eyes filling with tears.

"We go to England," he whispered. "Me and my brother. He jumped, but I am a coward. The truck rolled over him, and I ran away. I am too scared to call my mother. I cannot tell her that her oldest son is dead, and her youngest son is a coward. Now I have no phone."

"Sleep now," she said, "Things will look better in the morning."

He closed his eyes tight, squeezing out fat tears that ran down his cheek. "My mother will never forgive me. God will never forgive me."

"Nonsense," said Madame Marieke, wiping his eyes with a corner of the bedspread. "I don't know about God, but I know that your mother loves you. A mother will always love you, no matter what."

"No. It's been too long. I have waited too long and now it's too late."

"It's never too late," said Madame Marieke, though it rang hollow to her. "It's never too late," she repeated trying to control the quiver in her voice.

She let her hand drop to his shoulder, tucking the red chenille under his chin. A great welling was growing in her chest. She tried to resist its pull, but it was too strong. It tore at her heart, at every scab and scar that held it together. Madame Marieke sat, stroking his shoulder and hummed an old lullaby, relishing the memories of sleepy baby smell, until he fell asleep.

Back in her flat, Marieke tossed and turned all night while Lola snored contentedly at the foot of her bed. She wondered what his name was. She had forgotten to ask. She wondered what he might like for breakfast. She would get him some croissants, maybe some ham and cheese as well. She wondered if he would like one of those big puffy jackets? He certainly needed a jacket. And a hat and gloves. She would take him shopping in the morning. Maybe he could stay with her for a while? She had a spare room, and plenty of money saved over the years. She'd be getting her pension in a few years. Maybe it was time to retire. It would be nice to have someone to care for other than Lola and herself.

By the time dawn slipped in under the blind and seeped into her bedroom she had made a whole new life for them. One where she and Lola went to pick him up at school before going out for coffee and cake on a café terrace and spent Saturdays taking the tram to the park for a long walk around the lake.

The street was deserted in the early morning and looked like any normal street without the red and pink neon lights of the night trade. As Madame Marieke walked up to her building, she felt a sharp pinch of panic squeeze her heart. What if he was gone? What would she do with the dozen croissants she'd bought at the bakery, surprising the baker who had asked if she was planning a breakfast party? She let herself in and stood in the hallway, her heart pounding. Finally, she pushed open the door.

The room was empty.

The bed was neatly made, the cherry red chenille bedspread smoothed over the dip where his body had been.

Madame Marieke took a deep breath and sat down in her swivel chair, fumbling in her pockets for her cigarettes and lighter.

"So much for that," thought Madame Marieke. "*Tant pis*," she said out loud, not noticing the shake in her fingers as she lit a cigarette. "*Tant pis*," she repeated. It was what she had said as she walked away from the car where she handed over the swaddled bundle to the priest, who handed the baby over to an old nun sitting in the back seat. *Tant pis*. So much for that. Cecile was gone. The boy was gone. She still had Lola. She didn't even know the boy's name.

Madame Marieke opened the curtains and there he was - holding up a bag. "I went back to the park, and I found my bag. I could not see it in the dark," he said coming into the room. "I have my phone. I can call my mother. I need to tell her about my brother. Will you help me?"

"Yes. Of course, I will," she said, "but first you must tell me your name. And have breakfast! I bought croissants. Are you hungry?"

"My name is Yonas," he said, reaching out his hand, smiling. She took it, smiled back. And in his smile was hope. And in her smile was redemption. In their smiles was the forgiveness of all sins.

LISP 2023 Poetry Finalist
Jose Varghese

Midnight Hour

You sit on the floor
that's dusty
like in any students' hall,
your movements
so well-controlled
that you don't wake up
the other two boys, though
their snores
trouble you a lot.

You've closed
the Zoology record book,
kept it on the bed
with its half-finished
diagrams
of unicellular organisms,
prawns, sharks, vultures,
and human anatomy.

You place over it
a bunch of newsprint papers
and wait, pen in hand,
for a character
from the previous chapter
of your historical novel
to walk in,
each step accentuated
by the rustle
of her skirt over crinoline

and stand opposite you,
a dainty hand
on a hard-bound
Wuthering Heights
on the table,
smiling down
at your eyes that glow
in the light
of the brass wick lamp
that burns
between the two of you.

LISP 2023 Poetry Finalist
Sarah Boyd

Kitchen Sink Drama

A&E on a Saturday night
after chucking out time?
Honestly, you'd fit right in.
But here you are in my kitchen,
lurching towards me
like some kind of zombie,
arms rigidly outstretched,
satisfied smirk on your face.

Your T-shirt is black mixed
with apricot and pink,
drenched in crimson patches,
still wet, up your arms and
across your torso,
telltale dark crescents
under your nails.
I don't give you the satisfaction
of reacting, simply wait
for you to get cold and bored.

Later I plunge the top
into a bowl of water, tip it out.
The bloody liquid taints
the pure white basin
for a second, then
vanishes in a red tide
down the plughole.
'Til next time.

LISP 2023 Short Story Finalist
Rhiannon Lewis

The Waiter

In all the years we lived in that part of Fitzrovia, when Fitzrovia was still just a grubby backwater, there existed on the corner of Denbigh Street a Greek restaurant that we used to visit. We would go there at the end of a long or stressful day to pick up a takeaway. If we were being organised, we would order over the phone in advance. Mostly, we would turn up on spec and wait on uncomfortable benches while the chefs cooked our skewered chicken from fresh.

Chefs would come and go but, in all the years we frequented the place, there was only ever one head waiter. He supervised the takeaway counter whilst managing the serving of seated guests. He was a tall, rather heavily built man, not fat but neither was he genetically designed to flit elegantly between cramped dining tables. When he emerged from the kitchens with rows of plates balanced up each arm, there was a sense of impending disaster as if it was only a matter of time before his bulk, in such a confined environment, would lead to something being toppled or spilled.

Physically, he was not suited to his role, and you might be thinking to yourself that his welcoming personality or his charismatic repartee might have compensated for this unsuitability. He was, however, the least engaging waiter you'd ever meet.

He fascinated us, nonetheless, because over the years, we composed a catalogue of elaborate backstories for him. There were predictable fantasies involving Fitzrovia mafia, of which, incidentally, we knew nothing. We imagined him between jobs, waiting for a nod from his boss. Another time, we decided that he must have been a professional boxer, one win short of a dazzling career. His dour personality was the result of this damaging professional disappointment.

The petite waitress, who was of a similar age, occasionally stepped in to these scenarios. For a while, we had them down as husband and wife. But apart from exchanging sparse remarks about a side salad or the need for more glasses, we concluded that the body language didn't support our theory. Either that, or they'd divorced years earlier and like members of a too successful band were now forced to carry on singing together even though they hated each other's guts.

The years went by. The area changed. Depending on your perspective, it either began losing its character or emerged, butterfly-like from the grime. Old stonework was jet washed and windows replaced, ridiculously priced flats grew up from patches of billboarded wasteland. Pavements were landscaped and drums of elegant Amelanchier trees were installed on barren street corners. Corner cafes that had churned out bacon sandwiches with brown sauce and had been the haunt of off-duty taxi drivers began to sell expensive coffees from single estates. Tiled and listed shop fronts revealed themselves for the first time in years and were polished up. Our waiter (because over the years he had actually become *our* waiter) remained the same: efficient despite his ungainliness, serious, with very little to say for himself or for anyone else.

One evening, we returned to London, tired and emotionally wrung out by a long trip and a bereavement; I forget which trip and which bereavement, there have been so many by now. In any case, we made the decision to walk over to the Greek restaurant. Midweek, the place would be quiet and we relished the thought of being somewhere where no one would want to chat or ask us how we felt. We anticipated a straightforward meal, with starter and possibly dessert (did they even *do* dessert we asked ourselves), but definitely more rough wine than usual.

It didn't start well. We asked to be seated away from the door. It was a nasty evening and a perishingly cold wind was rattling all the signage and awnings along the street outside. Every time a customer came in to collect a meal, all the paper napkins took off like a flock of seagulls.

'Away from the door?' we repeated, shivering, and he looked us up and down. We were smart, for once, and our heavy coats might have given off the faint whiff of funerary mothballs.

He grunted in his usual non-committal way and bade us follow him around the corner and down a set of rickety stairs. When we reached the basement, there opened out before us a part of the restaurant we never knew existed. The room was entirely empty.

'There,' he said, and gestured towards a tiny table right next to a dark and glowering Christmas tree which, unlit, was like a sinister yuletide version of himself. He disappeared behind it for a moment. The tree quaked and the baubles trembled. Perhaps this was the moment we had anticipated for years, the moment of complete collapse, when tables and chairs and dishes would go flying in an Armageddon of debris. Then the fairy lights came on and our corner of the dismal basement was transformed. He even lit a candle and placed it in a shiny lantern.

'So, what will we be having this evening? Keftedes, moussaka, and a starter of calamari?'

It's true, we were creatures of habit, but we nearly fell off our chairs.

Yes, we replied, nervous as the tree baubles.

'And a bottle of the house red?'

No, we replied, reluctant to contradict him as he had spoken more words in one sentence than he'd used in all the years we had known him. No, we wanted a bottle of the Sigalas Santorini. We'd had a hard day, we added, apologetic.

The corner of his mouth curled upward very slightly, in what can only be described as a sneer.

'Huh,' he added and disappeared off to the kitchens.

The calamari arrived, the wine was opened and tasted, all in silence with only an occasional incoherent grunt from our waiter. Tucked away out of sight, embraced by the benevolent glow of the Christmas tree, we reflected on the unreal events of the previous days. Our lives had been usurped by shiny dark cars, black coats, carefully worded eulogies and uncomfortable shoes. The candle glowed steadily and we thanked our lucky stars that we were away from the draughty front door.

The first plates were cleared. The main meal arrived, all in characteristic silence. We congratulated ourselves on choosing the right restaurant for the occasion, a place where idle niceties were unnecessary and where we could be left in peace with our thoughts.

'Bill?' he asked, surprising us with his stealthy approach.

'Do you have any desserts?'

The baubles quivered. We cowered. He raised an eyebrow and produced a menu. Tiramisu seemed like a surprising offering for a Greek restaurant, but we weren't about to argue.

'Two of those, please.' We were pushing the boat out, reluctant to get back to shore as it were. We knew very well that our flat would be full of bitter reminders of how the world had once been. When you're young, you think of death as a kind of extraction, much like having a tooth removed. You imagine the hole in your life, but assume that everything around it will stay intact. No one ever warns you that it isn't about the hole at all but about everything else. The whole world changes. Dessert was a way of avoiding the archaeology, the ancient evidence of a hasty departure, a shoe left here, an essential phone charger left there; things that seemed to have happened a thousand years before.

The tiramisu turned up. We remarked how indulgent we were being, eating our own desserts rather than sharing. We ate slowly and ponderously, delving through the coffee layers, searching for evidence of liqueur.

We finished eating and wondered whether we should push the boat out even further and order some coffees. For how long would they tolerate us? It was warm and draught-free and we'd got attached to the tree. Our flat had been unheated for weeks.

Suddenly, sparkling lights appeared at the door. Our waiter was approaching with a pair of shot glasses which seemed to have disco balls flashing on their bases. He placed them down on the table.

'You're not from round here?'

An actual question, unrelated to food!

'No. But we've been here a while. Adopted.' We blurted over each other in shock.

'You know the BT tower?' he said.

We nodded.

'It's the anniversary today.'

'Of?'

'The explosion. Nineteen seventy-one.'

The disco lights inside the shot glasses took on the appearance of flashing police cars.

'I was a kid then. My dad owned this place and at four in the morning we heard an enormous explosion. Windows broken, debris everywhere.'

We glanced at each other and wondered where this was going. Despite his revelation, all our imagined scenarios came flooding back: mafia gang member, undercover gangster, decommissioned Russian spy, leader of a terrorist cell. Surely, he would have seemed more enthusiastic all these years if he'd been the owner rather than an employee? Away from the rest of the staff, was he just making it all up for entertainment? Later that evening, he might be catching the train back to his wife and six children, chuckling at the two dupes?

He went on to describe the panic, the police cordons and the increased security.

'They closed off the viewing platforms and it stopped being a tourist attraction. Business went downhill after that.'

We whistled. It was a long time for any business to be going downhill.

He gazed off into the middle distance as if he was x-raying the walls, waiting for some kind of enlightenment.

'You know those hoardings opposite?'

We nodded, but we weren't really sure.

'They're building expensive flats. Three point five million.'

We whistled again and made some comment about pointless gentrification.

The shot glass disco lights faltered and we wondered what lethal spirit was in store for us.

'Bill?' he asked, dragging his expectant eyes away from the walls.

We nodded, wide-eyed as our mouths exploded with vicious sweet liquid.

A little later, as we battled through the wind and rain, reeling slightly, we resolved, after all the years of living there, to ask his name.

'Next time we're there.'

It seemed odd that we didn't know.

'Even though he's grumpy.'

The weeks went by. The future lurched towards us, the way it does. We side-stepped the worst disasters, squared up to the head-on collisions as best we could. There were celebratory meals in other restaurants and poignant get-togethers on significant dates.

I find that, the older you get, meals have less and less to do with food.

Another long journey and a gruelling return, we decided that pork souvlaki with a side of tzatziki would perfectly fit our mood and bank balance. We headed out, on a warm, early spring evening, the sun just dipping below the rooftops but still glistening amber on the tall new office block windows.

We remembered our commitment to ask his name. After all these years, perhaps it was a sign that we were finally putting down roots. Had we, without realising it, already become Fitzrovians?

We rounded the corner, past the pub drinkers who were spilling on to the street. We walked the final stretch past the Thai restaurant that was being renovated, the tiny newsagent that was up for rent, and the brand new bakery we hadn't noticed before.

'Walnut, blue cheese and cracked pepper brioche. That sounds nice.'

The hoardings at the end of the street really had been hiding a block of expensive flats. They seemed to have sprung up overnight. Acres of glass and oddly shaped balconies wrapped around the block. According to the marketing blurb, there was a swish pool in the basement. We gazed enviously at the artist's impression of light-filled kitchens and thought of our own windowless cell with its deafening extractor fan.

When we got there, we thought the changing landscape had confused us; that somehow we had arrived at the wrong corner and that the Greek place was a block further on. We stepped into the street to survey the stretch of shops, just to make sure we weren't mistaken and were beeped at by a speeding moped.

'It's gone,' we chorused, flabbergasted. The sign had been dismantled, the windows had been changed, the steps had been reduced to a brand new ramp flanked by an arrangement of box trees in pots. The windows were screened off but there was a big notice on the door.

Opening soon. Wine bar and restaurant.

'We never got to find out his name!'

Between a row of parked cars, sat a fully laden skip, ready to be taken away. Peeking out from under the cover was the topmost branch of our Christmas tree, now withered, a shiny, cracked bauble still suspended in the shadows.

We took a detour and crossed Fitzroy Square, just to look at the beautiful buildings. Nothing much would be changing here. We circled the private gardens and wondered where *our* waiter was now. In a deckchair, we imagined, and smiling; sipping a glass of chilled Retsina, admiring his newly acquired vineyard, deep in conversation.

LISP 2023 Flash Fiction Finalist
Lynn Bushell

A Murderous Descent.

It was not a face that stood out from the crowd. He had ingenuous blue eyes, lips like a girl's. No friends. Nobody had owned up to being close to him. Perhaps some instinct told them that behind the mild front the unspeakable was happening.

Kohl looked for the photograph that said: 'This is the moment when it changed. But they weren't caught on camera. They took place in darkness, in the cellars of the mind or during sleep when nothing could prevent them coming to the surface.

Those on board had seven minutes from the moment when they knew that they were doomed. Kohl pictured infants screaming, mothers shielding children, fathers urging calm, and Bauer, the co-pilot, hammering against the cock-pit door, demanding to be let in. Bauer was a bully. Even his close friends admitted that.

They'd argued as the plane was getting ready to depart. A sandwich Bauer had asked Axel to collect from the canteen had pickle in it. Bauer hadn't wanted pickle in his sandwich.

'Axel hated being shouted at,' his mother said. 'When he was little he would run away and lock himself inside his room.'

Was that what he'd been doing as the plane descended at a rate of sixty feet a second on its murderous trajectory towards the north face of the mountain. Sixty seconds into the descent it would have been too late to alter course. It would take rescue teams weeks to gain access to the area and bring the bodies down, whilst in the cock-pit, his knees curled up underneath his chin, his eyes closed, Axel lay cut off from everybody, safe at last.

LISP 2023 Poetry Finalist
Kirk Millis-Ward

Pelham Woods

Along the creeping spring we wander
beneath broad oak and crowning pine
Our narrow path winds and falls
Aging limbs draped in healing time
Unburdened branches grasp at thoughts that flicker free
The strange fruit hanging there alone
is a facsimile of me

Bound by wild woodland
a world inside the cottage and a life against the cliff
Words built walls and probed for flaws
A marriage traced in hieroglyph
The cracks they found were illegible, unknowable and grand
Once carved in rock
promises we made were ground down into sand

Through such bitter substrate love's osmotic tendrils grow
The cottage in the wood
encasing emblem of this life and all we really know
Fresh blooms and fragrant glances

new love's story eager to be told
With trust and tender care
soft young leaves like souls unfold

LISP 2023 Short Story Finalist
Pat Ryan

The Days of Devil's Stew

Old lady Crawley used to tell fortunes but stopped when Leta disappeared. She won't read your palm now either for any amount of money. Not that she had any cause to be blamed for Leta.

Back when she told fortunes, a number of us girls would go to her house on the hill above the lake, some boys too. We called her Miz Crawley; nobody knew how old she was or if she'd ever been married.

This was known: Miz Crawley bought the abandoned Deer Lake Restaurant at a bankruptcy auction, moved right in and lived there alone. The shingled wood building wasn't in great shape, but it had a wrap-around porch, a big outdoor fireplace, a shed filled with firewood and a real nice view.

She nailed a sign on a tree at the dirt path that wound from the lake up to the house:

"Welcome. No booze. No drugs.
Fortunes told, $5 for 5 minutes."

She swore she never predicted what was going to happen to anyone, good or bad. “I can only give advice,” she said.

The first time I went, I tagged along with Leta. She gave Miz Crawley $5 and said she was in despair. She asked, “What will become of me in life?”

“I can only give advice,” Miz Crawley replied. Leta said that was the most boring remark she had ever heard. Nevertheless, she hung around the place. She must have felt some relief or comfort there because she kept returning.

Before long, Leta was practically living on the hill, in the house encircled by evergreens. The view across the lake to the cliffs beyond was, as my dad used to say, “worth the price of admission.”

There was a rhythm to those days, that time in my life, which synchronized with spring and summer. In the fall, I seldom visited, and never in winter. We weren’t always allowed. Miz Crawley was observant about the wildlife, watchful of what was happening on the ground and in the air. She wasn’t motivated by fear, for herself or for us, she was respecting the animals.

I bumped into her in town in late January, and she said, “It’s coyote mating season. I heard the howling last night, loud and long, like blues under the full moon." They don't howl because they want to eat us, she said, pointing a finger at my stomach. "They howl to find their coyote mates."

In April she said we could come back, so I trundled up to the house again. I was one of the first, followed by the other regulars, bigger and older now. Some, like Leta, had graduated from high school; others, like me, had one more year to go. We were on the verge of everything.

I was there when Miz Crawley and Leta made a pact. "If you take care of the grocery shopping and cooking," Miz Crawley said, "I'll help you find what you are looking for in life."

Was she a good person to teach a young woman about life? I couldn't say. The facts of *her* life, as she revealed them, provoked a series of questions and interpretations.

"I was born in these woods," she said, "nestled in an old fox's den." She was an orphan, she told us, raised by a Maine coon cat, "one of the gentle giants." A framed color photograph of a very big cat hung on the wall inside the entrance to the house. This cat had a leonine neck ruff, and one eye had two colors — exactly like Miz Crawley's — the iris was blue with orange patches. She was proud of that eerie likeness.

One of her adages was "Animals make the best mothers."

I tried to imagine my mother as an animal. A red fox might be nice, I thought, but a rabbit would probably be closer to her personality. A soft white rabbit.

Leta's mother, her real mother, had died in an accident when Leta was 10 years old. When her father died a year later, Leta was adopted by an elderly, childless couple. They were not the worrying kind and accepted her drifting away. They had expected it, though perhaps not quite so soon.

One of the boys said maybe Miz Crawley and Leta were related. They were both motherless and mysterious, he said. I'm sure they were not related, but nothing would have surprised me about either of them.

Leta began to cook. She started wearing an apron she found from the Deer Lake Restaurant. (Miz Crawley refused to wear it.)

On summer afternoons, our core group might laze around on the lawn and watch the sky turn to dusk. On these evenings, Leta would make what she called Devil's Stew. Her recipe was simple: mix olive oil, garlic and tomatoes with whatever was on hand (donations were encouraged). Spaghetti, linguine or chickpeas might be the main ingredient; on special occasions, fresh shrimp. Then she would spice it up, way up.

She liked to give orders: find kindling, build a log tower in the fireplace, get the fire blazing, set out the bowls and spoons. In a cast-iron pot, she would heat olive oil, onions and garlic (lots), add tomato paste, crushed tomatoes, oregano, salt and pepper, then chili or red pepper flakes, chili oil and even crushed chilis — until I made her stop.

One time she put extra chili oil on a boy's pasta because he had laughed at my skinny legs. I was wearing a new raspberry miniskirt and polka-dot crop top — the height of high school fashion. He went home early.

After the eating and washing up came the fortunes. Miz Crawley did not use any divination doodads but would sit and talk to her guests — that's what she called us, even after we paid our $5 — sometimes examine our palms or feel our head bumps, and tell short (exactly five minutes) stories filled with notions and metaphors, ending with choices, which ranged from benignly obvious to bluntly tart.

"What is past is past," she said to a young man I thought was rather cute. He was impatient to avenge his hurt pride. "Do not act like a knave," she told him. "Abandon the foolishness you are planning, stand straight and don't look back."

To a teenage girl with lush auburn hair, she said: "Do not weep because you are no longer a pious maiden. Your future is not foretold." She examined the girl's palm and said, "You have envy, yes, but not evil. Your true self is still there, waiting inside you."

When it was my turn, she said, "You, the quiet one, must find the words to make your choices." For my closing directive, she said, "Don't follow the obvious route. Explore life. Go to the source, depend on nothing but the original."

I didn't understand it at all.

We asked her for explanations. We wanted to know about love and marriage and children, but especially love. On that topic, Miz Crawley would not give any advice, saying simply, "Beware of misalliances."

She did like to talk. She had an articulate style that demanded attention and credence. Occasionally, she made general pronouncements. This one was a favorite:

"Your life will be like planting a seed that you fertilize and water, and you will grow up to be beautiful."

How do I "grow beautiful," I wanted to know.

At that, she laughed and said, "Baby, sometimes it's just luck, which never comes your way no matter what."

I believe that we were normal teenagers for our day. Our conversations were loaded, almost drunk, with talk of sex, with flaunts about admirers and seductions, with debates about the fine points of certain individuals.

"You should start howling to the hills," Miz Crawley would say to us.

At the end of every night, she would thoroughly douse the fire. This duty she kept for herself and would never go to bed until every ember was dead black. "No forest fires in my future," she said.

I did once get her to respond to my question about the lovers she had known. Dinner was over, and I was sitting beside her on the porch. She was in her rocker, drinking apple juice spiked with vodka. (I had noticed a Smirnoff bottle in the freezer.)

"I traveled far and wide to learn the secrets of the life force," she said. "No smooth, synthetic Americans, of any stripe, were allowed in my bed."

I urged her on.

"There was an Italian man I joined up with," she said. I remember her exact words, especially the phrase, "joined up with."

Her desire had been to learn Italian and read Dante's "Divine Comedy" in the original. And she did, but wouldn't spill further details. "Enough about all that, Baby," she said. Both she and Leta called me "Baby." I didn't mind, except when I wanted to know things.

She stepped down to check the fire. Peering into the flames, she whispered, "Inferno, Purgatorio, Paradiso."

At those words, the fire crackled, and sparks burst out of the wood. Everyone there jumped back. (Later, one of the girls claimed that Miz Crawley had poked the logs.)

......

Throughout July, Leta shopped, cooked, cleaned and gave orders. Miz Crawley took advantage of the free time and advertised her fortune-telling in the newspaper. I watched people of all ages and types come to her house. She made quite a bit of money that month.

We laughed at those middle-agers who expected to find out what their future held. What about our future? We no longer cared. We would never grow old — that was a myth. Jokes were made about who in the senior class was "the most likely to succeed."

Later, the auburn-haired girl said she thought I was the most likely. Surprised, I asked her why, and she said, "You have smart eyes. You must be thinking a lot."

One evening in August, when I was too tired to stay late — sweating from the day's lingering heat and the chili peppers in the Devil's Stew — I looked for Leta to see if she would walk back with me. I saw her by the fire, unmoving and staring, not into the smoldering fire, but into the darkness.

"This is not what I want to be," she said. "I can't stay here any longer."

Miz Crawley was standing in front of the house. She didn't speak. (And I didn't dare.)

That was the night Leta slipped away. It was the last time she was seen by anyone.

Leta's parents had no idea where she went. She was an adult, they said, with her own money and automobile.

Miz Crawley had no advice.

A new sign was posted at the dirt path that wound along the lake up to the house:

"No more fortunes will be told."

I went up anyway. Miz Crawley was rocking in the chair on the porch. Despite the warmth of the September afternoon, she wore a fluffy mohair scarf around her neck. It covered her ears and draped down to her chest, giving her a regal lionesque look.

Without greeting me, she began to talk. I listened in my quiet way.

"I wanted that bossy girl to go," she said. "I pushed her out of the nest — as an animal mother would — told her to fly out into the world, make her choices and try her luck."

As I rose to leave, she handed me the book she had been reading, a leather-bound volume of "La Divina Commedia." It had been autographed by Marcello.

"Take it," she said. "Many years from now, when you're midway in the journey of your life, you might find yourself in a dark wood."

She started rocking the chair, punctuating the finish. (There was no charge.)

The sound of a motorboat on the lake echoed around us. Here and now, all was bright, not a cloud in the sky. And yet, I shivered. I was beginning to understand things.

The rhythm changed again. Maybe it was due to the arrival of autumn or the ending of high school or the disappearance of Leta. What had once seemed an intriguing refuge now seemed a childish hideaway. I considered the possibility that the mystical mood of those days had been my imagination. But no, I could visualize the pot of stew, taste the spices and feel the heat on my tongue.

I confess that I miss the Devil's Stew most of all.

LISP 2023 Flash Fiction Finalist
Ros Thomas

Past Mortem.

As I rounded the corner, three things caught my eye: the lump of white sheet on the lawn, the swarm of police, the orange tape fluttering between the trees. Neighbours in dressing gowns stood in clumps by the curb, backlit by a weak sun. Their hot breath vaporised in pretty clouds as they stamped their feet and hugged themselves against the early morning cold. I slowed to a trot, then a walk, then loitered by the kerb, straining to hear the talk drifting from their huddle.

'It's that fella at number 6. Went out to get his paper.

Attacked?

Out the front. Throat slit, left to die.

Sweet Jesus.

Horrific. And one ear missing. Apparently.

Missing?

The cops can't find it.

Oh God. Like that bloke the other week? The one they found by the lake? He was missing one ear wasn't he?

That's what the papers said.

So it’s a serial killer?

Possibly.

Collecting trophies?

Looks that way.’

A bus rumbled up the street, swinging wide to pass the commotion, blocking my view of the crime scene. I stared up at its clumsy green bulk and locked onto its single passenger — a woman, window seat, halfway back, solid looking, mop of auburn hair.

As the bus slid by, she held my gaze, raised one hand to press something small and pink against the window. A flower maybe?

It took me a moment to register.

It was an ear.

And then the bus paraded her past me and accelerated away.

LISP 2023 Flash Fiction Finalist
Caitlin Magnall-Kearns

Stew and Dumplings

It had been twenty-two years since Jenny and Graeme had seen one another. When Jenny got Graeme's email, she ignored it for a week. And then, in the middle of another sleepless night, she plucked up the courage to open it. He was back in Belfast, and he wanted to see her.

Neither were Adonises to begin with, but as the years ticked along, their hair greyed and their edges softened. Jenny was worried he wouldn't like her now, her bingo wings and vast rolling hips. Graeme was self-conscious of his middle-aged spread. Of his short, dumpy legs and double chin. Both were aware of their many saggy, flabby bits that used to not be quite as saggy, or flabby.

She suggested dinner at hers, nothing fancy, beef stew and dumplings. He offered to bring a few bottles of wine and a pudding, Marks and Spencer's Tarte Au Citron. Jenny tried to not show how thrilled she was when he asked if he could stay the night. It meant he could have a drink and then drive home the next day.

"I don't see why not. I'll make up the spare bed"

Best to play these things cool, she thought. And besides, when he gets here he might not like what he sees.

When she opened the door she felt relieved. He had weathered as she had, aged

and widened as she had. He was just happy her eyes sparkled as they once did.

Later that night, when they went to bed together, all of their shared insecurities and hang-ups and "might have been" melted away. Neither one had to prove anything now. No, instead, they could just be.

Afterwards, they sat nude in bed, enjoying their tart as they talked about the news.

LISP 2023 Poetry Finalist
Mark Fiddes

Timewardens

Sitting in a hat with a shopping bag, I pass as one of the old boys
who collect faint as lint on benches in the town's pockets to study time.
In winter, we only need an hour if a blue sky coaxes out thin bees
for the pallid blossoms that burst too early from Council planters.
Another hatted man lowers himself beside me with a kind comment
about the weather - soon four of us balance on our stone bough.
One sucks his teeth at a horse's clop. The smoker taps ash into his hand.
The last brings a dog who hops into the space the atoms left behind.
Around us, Earth glides into place with pendulums, counterweights,
flywheels and a whisper of silicon. Somewhere a countdown has begun.
Our skin stretches, pulses quicken, as we advance headlong beyond
recorded speed into the eternal dimension of the present moment.

This could be the deck of a starship or the craggy edge of an asteroid hanging from the belt of Orion as we watch a pink ice cream van being dragged onto to a transporter from the parking enforcement office, burbling a gallows *Greensleeves*. Pleased with their morning, the hi-vis operatives lick their stolen 99's with flakes like porn stars. Whoever Mr. Whippy is, or was or promised to be, he has disappeared to a parallel universe or Burger King, whichever is the closer for lunch. We rise, lighting up, sucking teeth, patting the dog, agreeing to bump into each other again for tomorrow's installment.

Biographies

Amal Chatterjee, from various places including India, Sri Lanka, Scotland, and Amsterdam, has published fiction, history and commentary, and writes plays too. He divides his time between Amsterdam and Oxford and, besides writing, teaches fiction at Oxford University, in Amsterdam, Paris, Prague, Nepal, and elsewhere. He's been shortlisted for prizes in India and the UK, and judges some too.

Of Maltese origin (b.1982) **Karina Fiorini** lives in France. Her poetry features in Modern Poetry in Translation, PEN Malta and PEN International and Les Cahiers Luxembourgeois, amongst others. La Moselle, an editor's choice is published in Survival Anthology by Hammond House Publishing. Her writing explores time, loss, human frailty and the environment. Karina is presently working on her first poetry collection. www.karinafiorini.com

Gillian O'Shaughnessy is a journalist and writer from Walyalup, Fremantle. She has work in SmokeLong Quarterly, Fractured Lit, Best Small Fictions 2023 and Jellyfish Review among others. You can find her at gillianoshaughnessy.com

Jess Richards is the author of three literary fiction novels which are published by Sceptre, and most recently a creative nonfiction book, Birds and Ghosts, published by Linen Press. She also writes short stories which have been published in various anthologies. With a background in visual performance and writing from Dartington College of Arts, her experimental writing often edges the boundaries between poetry and prose, text and image, art and writing.

Kwame MA McPherson is a co-author and Amazon best seller for 'The Heart of a Black Man' anthology. He is the Commonwealth Short Story Prize 2023 Winner, for the Caribbean region and Globally, the first Jamaican to win this type of literary competition. Kwame is a book coach and ghostwriter.

Ivy Raff is the author of What Remains / Qué queda (Editorial DALYA, forthcoming 2023), winner of the Alberola International Poetry Prize, and Rooted and Reduced to Dust (Finishing Line Press, forthcoming 2024), hailed by Bruce

Smith as "lacerating, fearless." Ivy has backpacked through 74 countries and lived abroad in Dominica.

London-based Architect and writer **Tunde Oyebode** is interested in capturing the subtleties of daily life in his fiction. His other works appear in Stylist (Online), Obsidian Magazine Issue 48.1, and the 2021 Michael Terrence Anthology. He's also received acclaim in the Chester B Himes Memorial Fiction Contest and the Bristol Short Story Prize.

Sue Harper has published many books on British cinema, and in 2020 Egaeus Press published her collection of short stories, "The Dark Nest"

Alison Grove lives and works in the NW Highlands of Scotland. Her short fiction has appeared in a number of journals and collections, including The MacAllan Scotland on Sunday Collection, Fish Anthologies, and broadcast as part of the Commonwealth Short Stories on BBC Radio 4.

Gina Challen lives in West Sussex. She holds a MA in Creative Writing. She is published in anthologies, online, shortlisted for the Bridport Prize, longlisted for the RSL, V S Pritchett Prize and a finalist in the 2021 LISP. Her collection, Chalk Tracks, is published by Valley Press. WWW.ginachallen.co.uk. @ginabchallen

Laurie Bolger is a London based writer & founder of The Creative Writing Breakfast Club. Laurie's Poetry & Short Stories have featured at Glastonbury, across BBC Platforms, Sky Arts & TATE. This year she was awarded The Moth Prize & her Flash Fiction was shortlisted for The Bridport Prize.

Hannah Stephings is a writer, youth worker and trainee psychotherapist, based in Edinburgh. She is a Pushcart Prize nominee and her work has featured both in print and online in The Loft Book Anthology, Horse Egg Literary Review, TAST zine and SNACK magazine amongst other publications.

Linda Jorgenson is a retired businesswoman who holds dual American and British citizenship. She currently lives in England. Her flash fiction memoir piecc was published in Mslexia magazine, she's been long-listed for a Fish

Publishing Award, completed a Faber writing course, and has finished her debut novel, Second Favourite.

Fiona Dignan is a writer of poetry, flash and microfiction. Winner of the Plaza Prize for Sudden Fiction and The London Society Poetry Prize. She has been placed in several competitions including Reflex, Retreat West and Propelling Pencil and has featured in numerous magazines and anthologies including Mslexia and Popshot.

Niles Reddick is author of a novel, three collections, and a novella. His work has been featured in over 500 publications including The Saturday Evening Post, New Reader Magazine, The Museum of Americana, Citron Review, Nunum, Right Hand Pointing, and Vestal Review. He is a four-time Pushcart, three-time Best Micro, and three-time Best of the Net nominee.

Tina Pisco is a writer of novels, newspaper columns, poetry and short stories. In 2020/21 she became the first Writer-in-Residence for Cork City Libraries, and in 2021/22 was awarded the prestigious Frank O'Connor Fellowship by the

Munster Literature Centre. Her first short story collection (Sunrise Sunset and other fictions, FISH 2016) was long listed for the Edge Hill Prize.

Jose Varghese was a finalist in the 2018 Beverly International Prize, runner up in the Salt Prize, commended in the Gregory O'Donoghue Prize, finalist twice in LISP, published in Litro, Nine Arches Press, Haunted Waters, Southword, Camas, Dreich, Wild Roof, Meridian APWT/Drunken Boat, Unthology, Reflex Fiction, and Flash Fiction Magazine.

Sarah Boyd read History at the University of Exeter and for many years worked in magazine journalism and production. She rediscovered the joys of poetry during lockdown and regularly participates in poetry open mics in her local area.

Rhiannon Lewis is an award-winning Welsh writer. Her debut novel was recommended by the Walter Scott Prize. She was runner-up in the New Welsh Writing Awards in 2019, the winner of the William Faulkner Short Story Prize in 2020 and shortlisted for the Wales Book of the Year in 2022.

Lynn Bushell is a painter and author. Her latest novel 'Painted Ladies' (2019 was published by Sandstone Press. Her short stories have twice been longlisted for the Commonwealth Prize and have been awarded prizes by The London Magazine Short and Flash Fiction 500.

Kirk Millis-Ward is a neurodivergent poet and author who lives in a cottage by the sea with his wife and young son.

Pat Ryan's stories have been published in the literary journals Chautauqua, American Writers Review, The Ghost Story, The Hopper, and Cleaver Magazine. Her articles on movies, music, and literature have appeared in The New York Times, where she was an editor in the Culture Department. She lives in Deerfield, Massachusetts.

Ros Thomas is a journalist turned author. After twenty years in television she became a long-running newspaper columnist then turned to fiction. Her first novel How To Shame The Devil became a West Australian best seller. Her flash fiction won the UK Staunch Prize in 2021.

Caitlin Magnall-Kearns is an award-winning queer, disabled writer from East Belfast with a passion for telling unheard and underrepresented stories. She works across writing for page, stage, screen and audio, and is currently writing her third commission for BBC Radio 4.

Mark Fiddes is a writer based in the Middle East and Spain. His most recent collection of poetry is 'Other Saints Are Available' (Live Canon). He is a winner of the Oxford Brookes International Prize, the Ruskin Prize and the Westival Prize and is published widely in poetry journals and newspapers.

LISP
LONDON
INDEPENDENT
STORY PRIZE

2023